START YOUR ENGINES!

4X4 TRUCKS

By Martha London

Kaleidoscope
Minneapolis, MN

The Quest for Discovery Never Ends

This edition first published in 2020 by Kaleidoscope Publishing, Inc.

For information regarding permission, write to
Kaleidoscope Publishing, Inc.
6012 Blue Circle Drive
Minnetonka, MN 55343

Library of Congress Control Number
2019940173

ISBN
978-1-64519-051-6 (library bound)
978-1-64494-209-3 (paperback)
978-1-64519-152-0 (ebook)

Printed in the United States of America.

Bigfoot lurks within one of the images in this book. It's up to you to find him!

TABLE OF CONTENTS

Chapter 1: Mud Is No Problem 4

Chapter 2: Go Anywhere, Do Anything 10

Chapter 3: Grip the Ground 16

Chapter 4: Farm, City, Desert 22

Beyond the Book 28

Research Ninja 29

Further Resources 30

Glossary 31

Index 32

Photo Credits 32

About the Author 32

CHAPTER 1

Mud Is No Problem

The **4x4** truck thumps over the rough ground. Ben goes slowly. He drives through deep ruts. His truck has no problem. Its tires have thick grooves. They help the truck grip the road.

Ben comes up to a mud puddle. He can't see how deep it is. He rolls up the truck's windows. He steps on the gas pedal. Fuel surges through the engine. Power flows to the **axles**. The truck's wheels spin faster. The truck speeds toward the mud.

Having a 4x4 truck that can go through deep mud puddles is important for off-road adventures.

ZOOM IN ON A 4X4 TRUCK

Splash! Mud covers the truck's hood. Brown water splatters everywhere. Ben sprays his windshield to clean it. He continues down the dirt road.

More rocks and boulders fill the path. The ride is even bumpier than it was before. Each wheel moves separately over the rough road. The tires are made of thick rubber. Sharp rocks won't tear holes in them.

Rocks, boulders, and other obstacles are no match for a 4x4 truck's tires and four-wheel drive.

Ben reaches a hill. It's steep. He revs the engine. He needs more power to climb the hill. But he doesn't want to go too fast. One of the rocks could flip the truck over.

Ben pauses at the top of the hill. Then he speeds down the hill. He skids around sharp corners. He finally pulls out of the woods. His truck is caked in thick, brown mud.

Layers of mud on a 4x4 truck show off its abilities.

Tiny spots of red paint shine through on the roof. Everywhere else is covered in mud.

Ben loves mudding. He's proud of the layers of grime. They show that his truck can go through anything. He gets home in time for dinner. He uses a hose to clean his truck. The dirt melts off. Next weekend, Ben will try a new spot.

FUN FACT

Mudders often keep their tire pressure a little low to increase their trucks' grip on the ground.

CHAPTER 2

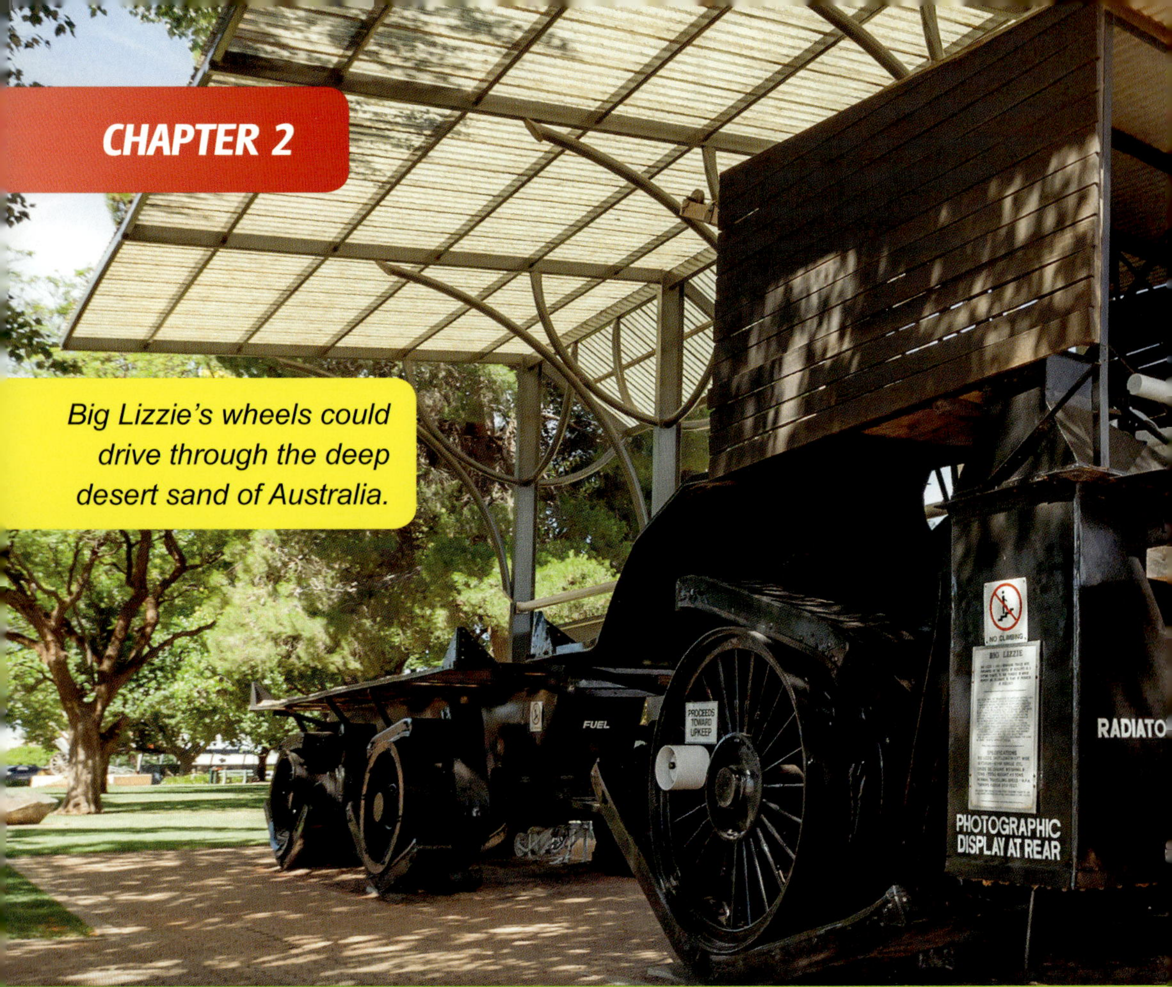

Big Lizzie's wheels could drive through the deep desert sand of Australia.

Go Anywhere, Do Anything

Frank Bottrill had a problem. Australia is full of deserts. Wheels get stuck in the deep sand. People used camels to carry loads of wool and wheat. But Bottrill was sure there was a better way. He started building a truck.

Bottrill finished "Big Lizzie" in 1915. The name said it all. Everything about the truck was big. Big Lizzie weighed 45 tons (40 metric tons). But Big Lizzie was not fast.

FUN FACT

Big Lizzie is now on display for the public in Red Cliffs, Australia.

It plodded along at 1 mile per hour (1.6 km/h). Big Lizzie pulled two huge trailers behind it. They were loaded with wheat.

Big Lizzie's wheels moved over the sand easily. Huge, flat pieces attached to the wheels made sure the truck didn't sink. Big Lizzie inspired other automakers. They wanted their vehicles to be able to drive anywhere.

Early Jeeps were built for military use during World War II.

More 4x4 trucks were made in the next few decades. But most were for the military. The United States wanted new vehicles during World War II (1939–1945). It needed a truck to go everywhere and do everything. Two car companies worked together. Ford and Willys-Overland created the Jeep.

Soldiers could pile onto the Jeep's green fabric seats. They drove out to the battlefield. Injured soldiers needed to be picked up. Roads were rough. But the Jeep could handle it. It had thick rubber tires. Deep grooves gripped the rocky ground. There was no time to get stuck. People needed help.

After World War II, more people could buy their own 4x4 trucks. They weren't just for the military.

4X4 STATS:

2017 FORD F-150 XL

ENGINE SIZE	FUEL CAPACITY
6-cylinder	23 gallons (87 L)
TOWING CAPACITY	**WEIGHT**
Up to 12,200 pounds (5,534 kg)	Up to 4,932 pounds (2,237 kg)
TRANSMISSION	**SPECIAL FEATURES**
Automatic with tow/haul and sport modes	Four-wheel drive, underbody skid plates, and off-road-tuned front shock absorbers

A new truck came along in the 1980s. It was called the Humvee. Humvees are made for the military. They pull and haul. They're a lot like Jeeps. They can go over and through almost anything. Humvees are massive vehicles.

Car companies started selling the Hummer. It was a version of the Humvee for the public. The Humvee sped over desert sand. But the Hummer flew over asphalt. The Hummer started a movement toward bigger and more powerful trucks.

Hummers were available to the public and were based on Humvees, which are made for the military.

CHAPTER 3

Grip the Ground

Leah turns the key in the **ignition**. Fuel flows to the engine. The 4x4 truck roars to life.

Snow covers the road. Leah's truck is going to clear it. Snowplows are bigger than this truck. They clear city streets first. But this truck clears driveways and farm roads. It heads to the dirt roads outside town.

The snow is deep and heavy. Chains wrap around the truck's tires. These chains improve the truck's **traction**.

FUN FACT

Ford offered the first factory-built four-wheel drive trucks in 1959.

Snowplows clear city streets, but pickup trucks are often used to clear driveways, farm roads, and parking lots.

They help the wheels grip the slippery roads. Leah revs the engine. The wheels begin to spin. Leah is glad to have four-wheel drive. On some cars, the engine powers only two wheels. A 4x4 truck's engine powers all four wheels. This helps it drive on slippery roads. Leah can tell the roads are slick. But each tire grips a different part of the road. She has better traction.

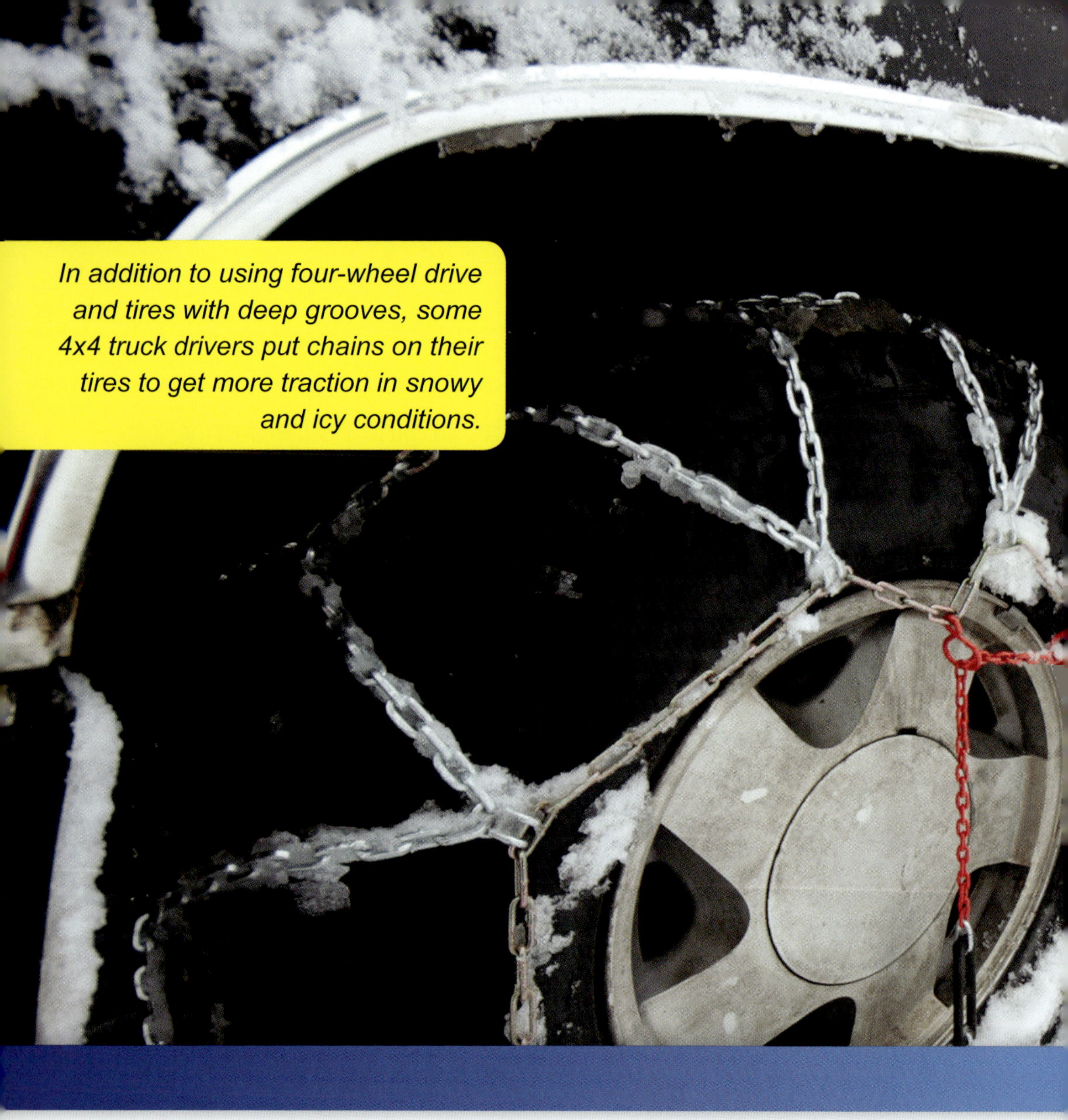

In addition to using four-wheel drive and tires with deep grooves, some 4x4 truck drivers put chains on their tires to get more traction in snowy and icy conditions.

Leah reaches her first driveway. It's long. Six inches (15 cm) of snow cover the gravel underneath. She puts the plow blade down. The blade is like a large shovel. It's attached to the front of the truck.

The truck's engine is big. It is powerful. The truck can carry and push more weight than a car can.

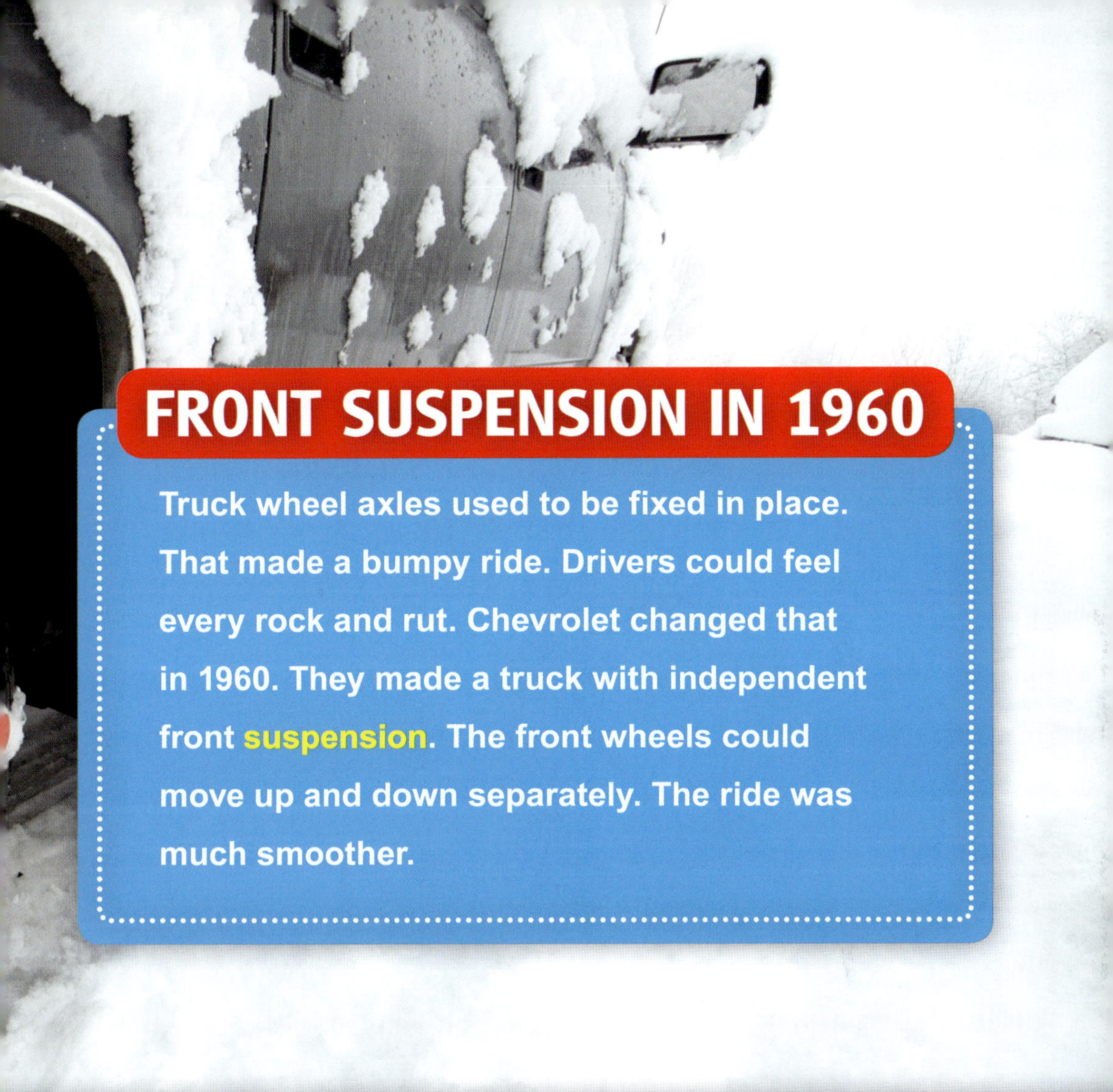

FRONT SUSPENSION IN 1960

Truck wheel axles used to be fixed in place. That made a bumpy ride. Drivers could feel every rock and rut. Chevrolet changed that in 1960. They made a truck with independent front **suspension**. The front wheels could move up and down separately. The ride was much smoother.

Leah drives forward slowly. Snow piles up in front of the plow. Huge drifts form. The shape of the driveway is showing through. Leah pushes the snow out of the way with the plow blade. The snow is heavy. But the truck's powerful engine keeps the truck moving.

HOW BIG IS A 4X4?

4X4 PICKUP TRUCK

Width
8 feet
(2.5 m)

Length
19 feet (5.8 m)

SEDAN

Width
6 feet (1.8 m)

FUN FACT

The Ford F-Series line has been the top-selling truck in the United States for over forty years.

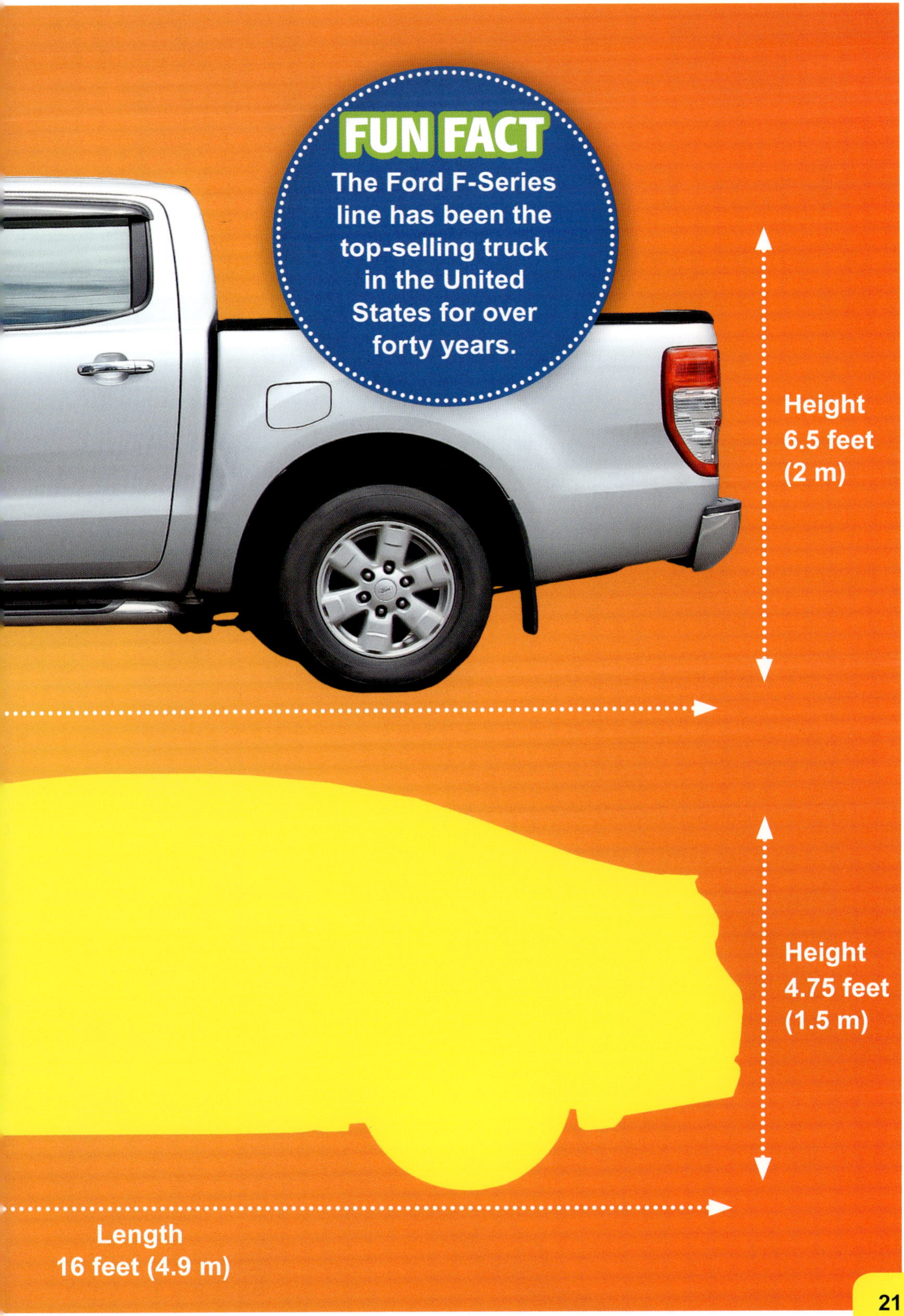

CHAPTER 4

Farm, City, Desert

Many 4x4 trucks have jobs to do. Some are used in emergencies.

An alarm sounds. There's no time to waste. The **paramedics** jump into the ambulance. Sirens blare as the garage door opens. Rain pours and thunder crashes. Water flows down the streets. But they still have to get to the patient.

Headlights show the way in the dark. Wiper blades clear the windshield. The paramedics are in the back. They make sure they have everything ready. Cabinets and drawers hold medicine and bandages. Blankets sit folded in overhead bins. A bed called a stretcher is in the middle.

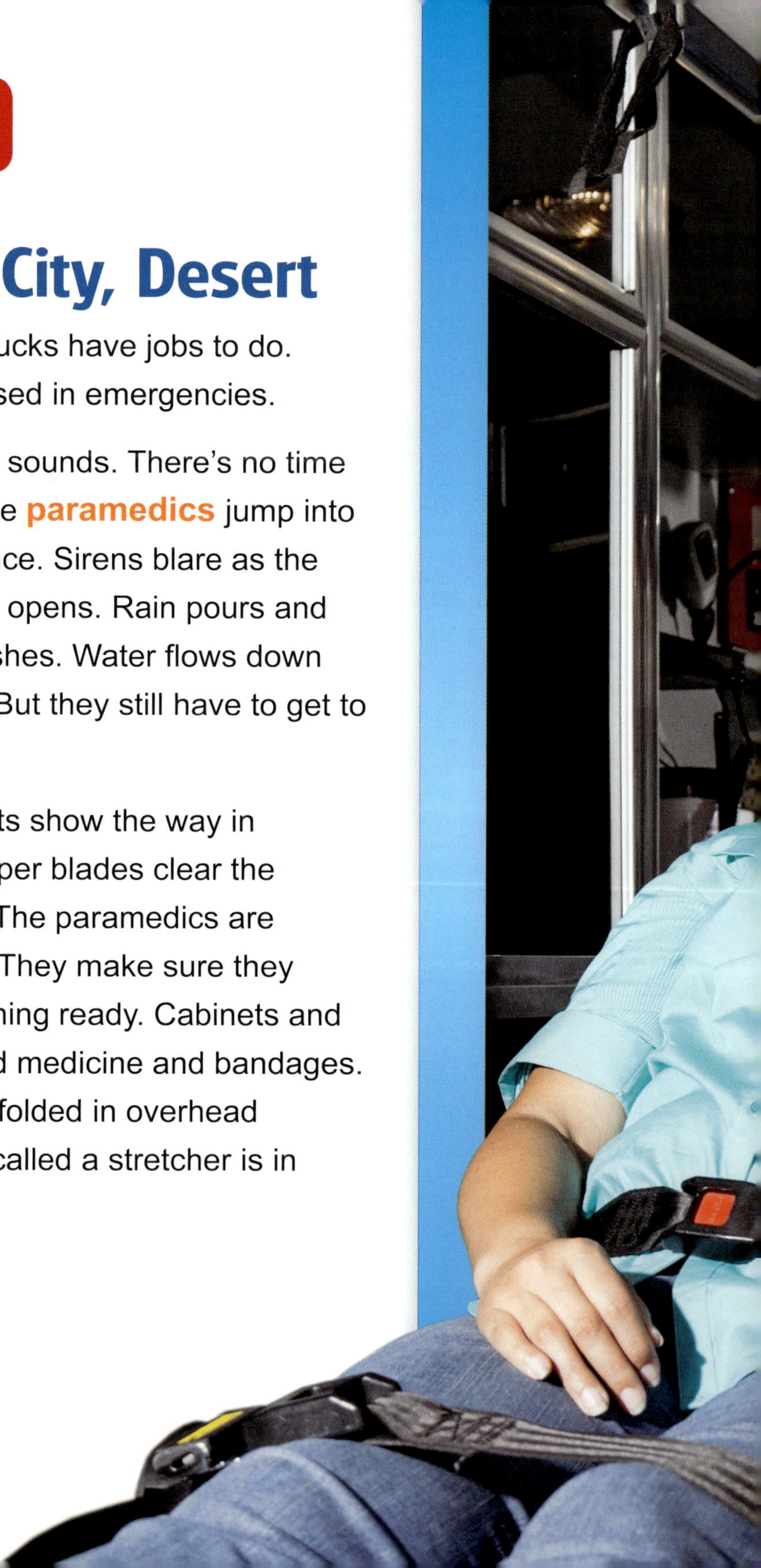

Many ambulances are 4x4 trucks so that they can drive more quickly in difficult conditions.

The driver goes as fast as he can. Power goes to the wheels. Some goes to the medical equipment too. All of the equipment runs on electricity. That energy comes from the truck battery. The engine charges the battery as the vehicle runs. The team has all the tools it needs to get the patient to the hospital safely.

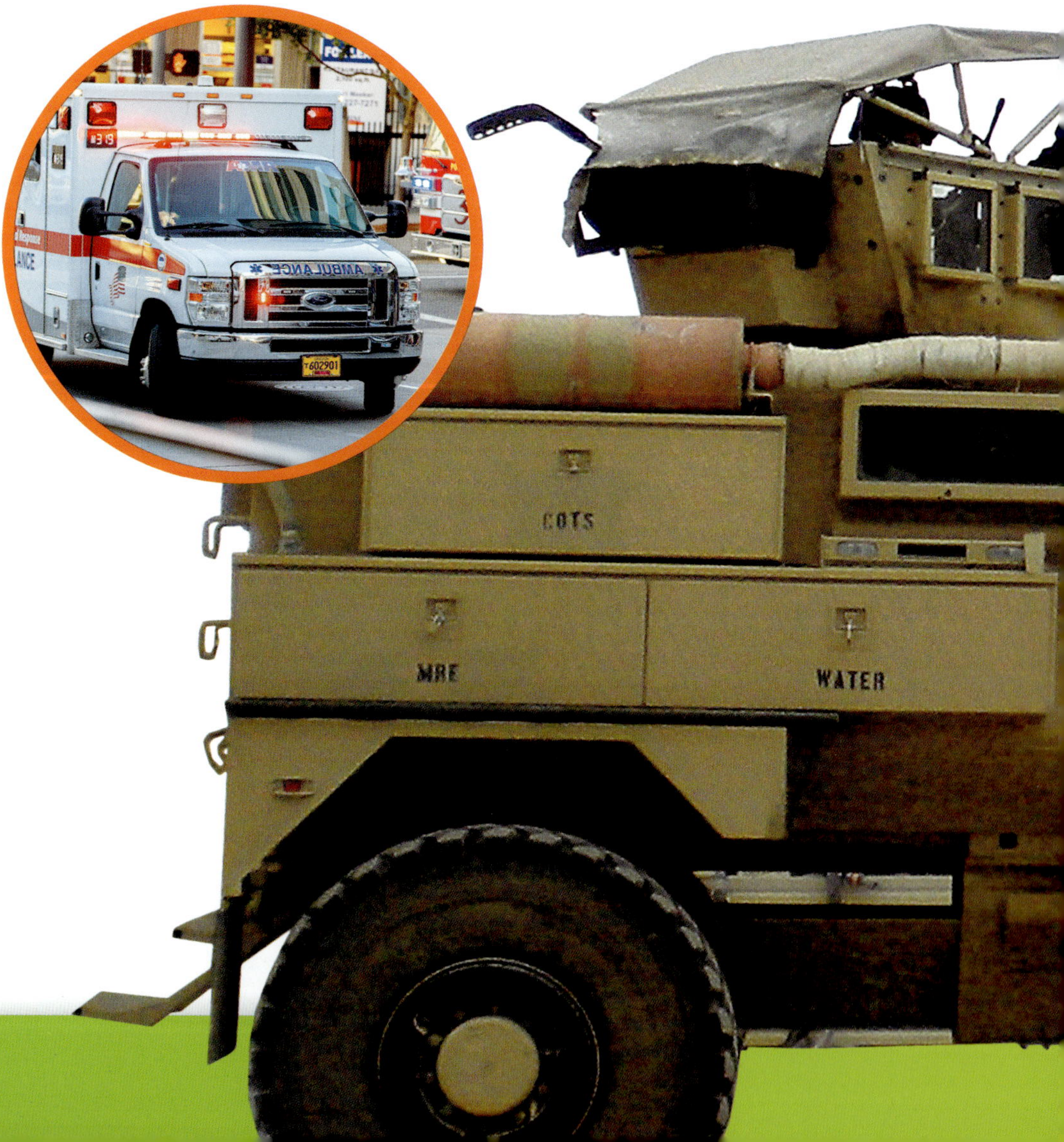

Other 4x4 trucks are used in the military. Out in the desert, vehicles need to be dependable. The soldiers are in their Cougar ISS. The truck's windows are small. Its sides are thick. They protect the soldiers from bullets. The soldiers are far away from cities and towns. The **terrain** changes. It goes from bumpy rocks to slippery sand. But that's no problem. The truck can handle anything.

Soldiers use Cougar 4x4 trucks on the battlefield because the thick sides protect them and four-wheel drive helps them through rough terrain.

Farmers use 4x4 trucks as well. A rancher in California backs up his 4x4. He lowers his trailer onto the **hitch**. The back of the truck sinks a little under the weight. He leads his horses into the trailer. The gate closes behind them.

The rancher hops in the cab of his truck. He rolls the windows down and starts the truck. The smell of fuel fills the air. He **accelerates** slowly. Dust kicks up behind him on the road. The truck can haul thousands of pounds.

Some 4x4 trucks can haul thousands of pounds, so they're an excellent choice for traveling with horses and other heavy animals.

The rancher has five horses traveling to Kentucky. The horses are being trained there. Each of them weighs 1,000 pounds (455 kg).

Four-wheel-drive trucks help people get their work done. They are powerful machines. They can haul heavy equipment and animals. They can drive in all kinds of weather. Their tires handle all kinds of terrain. There isn't much that can stop a 4x4 truck.

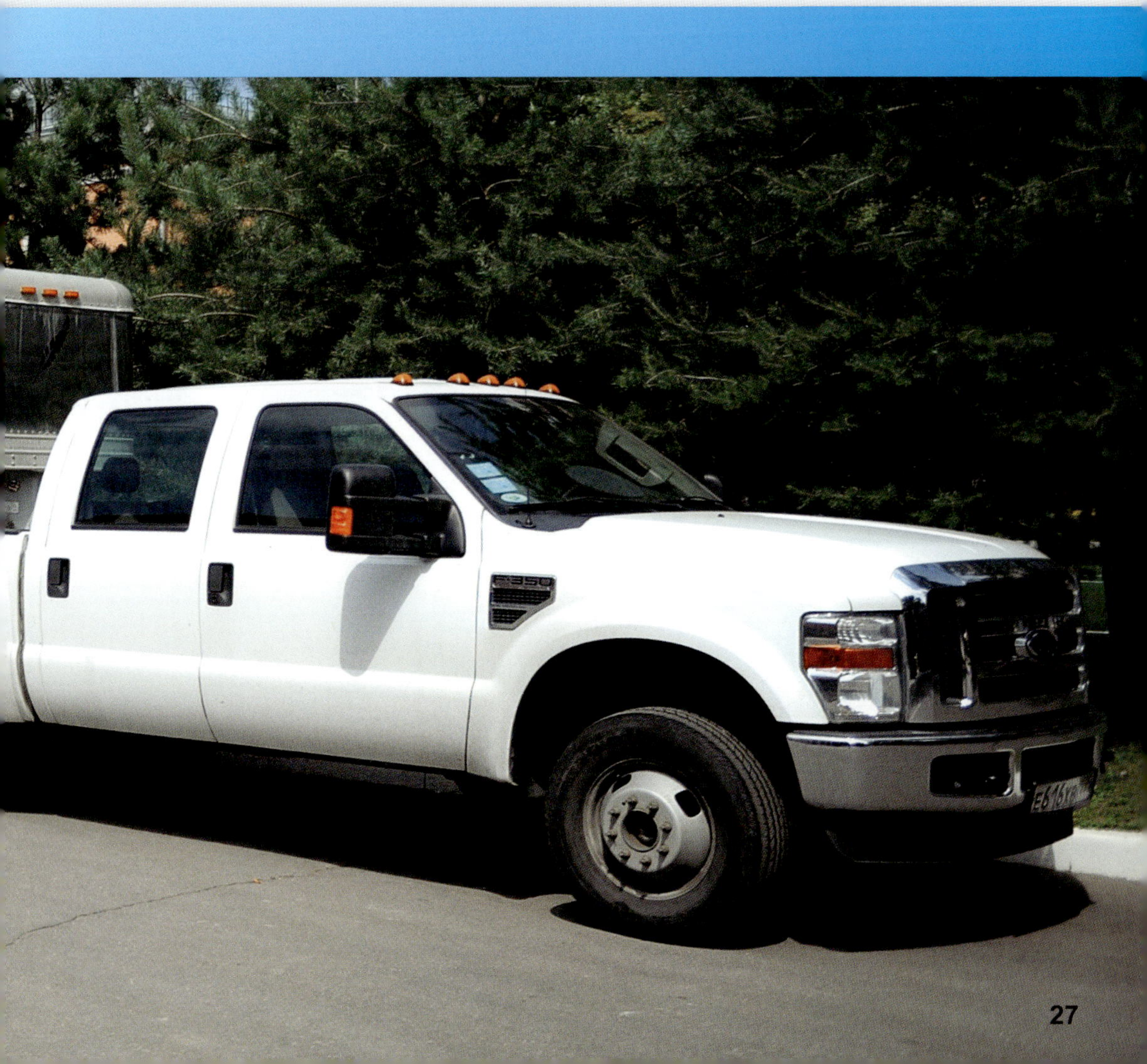

BEYOND THE BOOK

After reading the book, it's time to think about what you learned. Try the following exercises to jumpstart your ideas.

THINK

DIFFERENT SOURCES. What types of sources might you be able to find for more information about pickup trucks? How might an encyclopedia help you? What about a newspaper article? How is each source useful in its own way?

CREATE

PRIMARY SOURCES. Primary sources are first-hand accounts. They can include interviews, videos, and photographs. Create a list of the kinds of primary sources you might be able to find about 4x4 trucks.

SHARE

SUM IT UP. Write one paragraph summarizing the important points from the whole book. Make sure to write the summary in your own words—don't just copy from the text. Share the paragraph with a classmate. Does your classmate have any feedback on the summary or additional questions about 4x4 trucks?

GROW

REAL-LIFE RESEARCH. What kinds of real-world places could you visit to do more research on how much weight trucks can tow? What other topics could also be explored at this place?

RESEARCH NINJA

Visit www.ninjaresearcher.com/0516 to learn how to take your research skills and book report writing to the next level!

RESEARCH

DIGITAL LITERACY TOOLS

SEARCH LIKE A PRO
Learn about how to use search engines to find useful websites.

FACT OR FAKE?
Discover how you can tell a trusted website from an untrustworthy resource.

TEXT DETECTIVE
Explore how to zero in on the information you need most.

SHOW YOUR WORK
Research responsibly—learn how to cite sources.

WRITE

GET TO THE POINT
Learn how to express your main ideas.

PLAN OF ATTACK
Learn prewriting exercises and create an outline.

DOWNLOADABLE REPORT FORMS

Further Resources

BOOKS

Grack, Rachel. *Automobiles from Then to Now*. Amicus Ink, 2020.

Mack, Larry. *Chevrolet Silverado*. Bellwether Media, 2019.

Mack, Larry. *Ford F-150*. Bellwether Media, 2019.

WEBSITES

FACTSURFER

Factsurfer.com gives you a safe, fun way to find more information.

1. Go to www.factsurfer.com.
2. Enter "4x4 Trucks" into the search box and click 🔍.
3. Select your book cover to see a list of related websites.

Glossary

4x4: Four-wheel drive is often shortened as 4x4. Four-wheel drive is when an engine powers each wheel individually. Each wheel of the 4x4 truck grips the ground separately.

accelerates: When something accelerates, it goes faster. The truck accelerates around the curve.

axles: Axles are long metal poles that hold two wheels on a vehicle. If their trucks have fixed axles, drivers can feel every bump in the road.

cab: The cab of the truck is where the driver sits. The truck's cab had a lot of legroom.

hitch: A hitch is what connects a trailer to a truck. The truck needed a hitch so it could pull the camper.

ignition: The ignition starts an engine. The driver couldn't start the truck because the ignition switch broke.

paramedics: Paramedics are people trained to give emergency medical care to someone in need. Paramedics ride in an ambulance.

suspension: The suspension in a truck acts like a cushion against the bumps in a road. The truck has a great front suspension system, so it is a smooth ride.

terrain: Terrain is the physical features on the ground. The terrain was filled with rocks and bumps.

traction: Traction is when a vehicle's tires grip the ground. The truck had a hard time getting traction on the icy roads.

Index

ambulances, 22, 24
axles, 4, 19

Big Lizzie, 10–11

Chevrolet, 19
Cougar ISS, 25

engines, 4, 8, 14, 16–17, 18–19, 24

Ford, 13, 14, 16, 21
four-wheel drive, 6, 14, 16, 17, 27

hauling, 11, 14, 15, 26–27
Hummer, 15
Humvee, 15

Jeep, 13, 15

military, 13, 15, 25
mudding, 4, 6, 8–9

ranchers, 26–27

size, 20–21
snow plowing, 16–19
suspension, 19

tires, 4, 5, 6, 9, 10, 11, 13, 16–17, 19, 24, 27
traction, 9, 16–17

Willys-Overland, 13

PHOTO CREDITS

The images in this book are reproduced through the courtesy of: contrastaddict/iStockphoto, front cover (truck); Doidam 10/Shutterstock Images, front cover (road); Ed Aldridge/Shutterstock Images, p. 3; Ovu0ng/Shutterstock Images, p. 4; Art Konovalov/Shutterstock Images, p. 5; The Len/Shutterstock Images, p. 6; Tramino/iStockphoto, pp. 6–7; SAMIphoto/iStockphoto, pp. 8–9; Photodigitaal.nl/Shutterstock Images, pp. 10–11; U.S. Army Signal Corps/Farm Security Administration/Office of War Information Black-and-White Negatives/Library of Congress, p. 12 (soldiers); Steve Lagreca/Shutterstock Images, pp. 12–13; Everett Historical/Shutterstock Images, p. 13; Ed Aldridge/Shutterstock Images, p. 14 (truck); Art Konovalov/Shutterstock Images, p. 15; pokergecko/iStockphoto, p. 16–17; RonBailey/iStockphoto, p. 18; nitinut380/Shutterstock Images, pp. 20–21 (top); Steve Lagreca/Shutterstock Images, pp. 20–21 (bottom); kali9/iStockphoto, pp. 22–23; Alexander Oganezov/Shutterstock Images, p. 24; Tim Daugherty/Shutterstock Images, pp. 24–25; Free Wind 2014/Shutterstock Images, pp. 26–27; Michael Shake/Shutterstock Images, p. 30.

ABOUT THE AUTHOR

Martha London lives and works in Minnesota. She writes children's books full-time. When she's not writing, you can find her hiking.